Thank you to the generous team who gave their time and talents to make this book possible.

Writer
Jane Kurtz

Creative Directors
Caroline Kurtz and Jane Kurtz

Illustrator
Katie Bradley

Designer
Sarah Richards and Beth Crow

Translator
Mastewal Abera

Ready Set Go Books, an Open Hearts Big Dreams Project

Special thanks to Ethiopia Reads donors and staff for believing in this project and helping get it started-- and for arranging printing, distribution, and training in Ethiopia.

THE RUNAWAY INJERA

ኮብላይ እንጀራ

English and Amharic

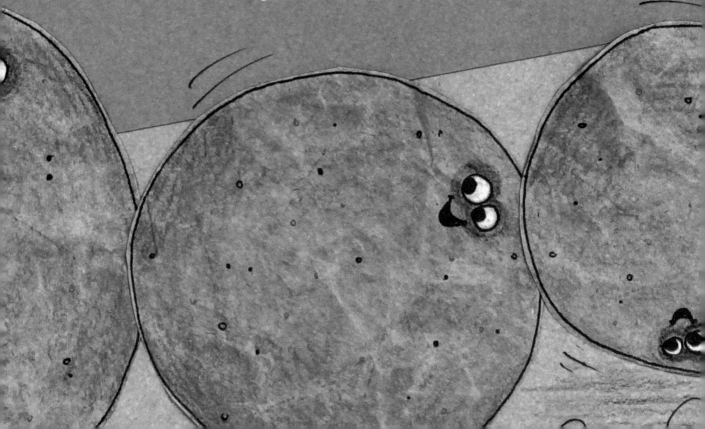

One day, a woman was putting an injera in her basket when it leaped out of her hands.

ከዕለታት አንድ ቀን አንዲት ሴት እንጀራ አውጥታ ወደመሶቡ ልታስቀምጠው ስትል ከእጇ ዘሎ አመለጠ።

It rolled across the floor and out the door.

በወለሉ ላይም ተንከባለለና በበሩ ወጣ።

"Stop!"
called the
woman. "You will
be soft and warm
to eat
today."

'ቄም!' አለቻው ሴትየዋ። 'ትኩስ
እንደሆንክ ዛሬውኑ ትበላለህ ።'

The injera called, "You have legs, but I am ROUND.
I roll zip-zip across the ground."

እንጀራውም 'አንቺ እግሮች አሉሽ እኔ ደግሞ ክብ
መሬት ላይ በፍጥነት እላለሁ ክብልልል' አላት።

The injera rolled along the street.

እንጀራውም በመንገዱ ዳር እየተንከባለለ ሔደ::

"Stop!" the people called.
"You will be soft and warm to eat today."

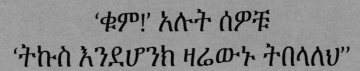

'ቁም!' አሉት ሰዎቹ
'ትኩስ እንደሆንክ ዛሬውኑ ትበላለህ"

The injera called, "You have legs, but I am ROUND.
I roll zip-zip across the ground."

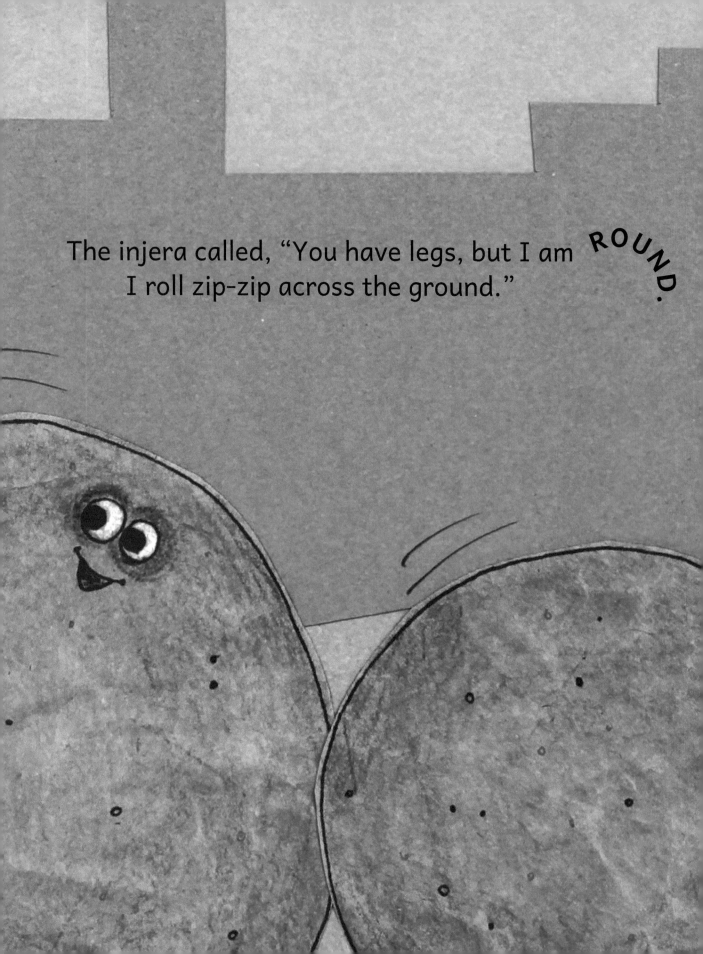

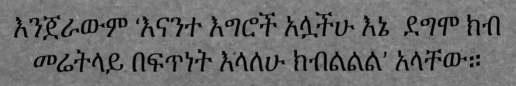

እንጀራውም 'እናንተ እግሮች አጪችሁ እኔ ደግሞ ክብ
መሬትላይ በፍጥነት እላለሁ ከብልልል' አላቸው።

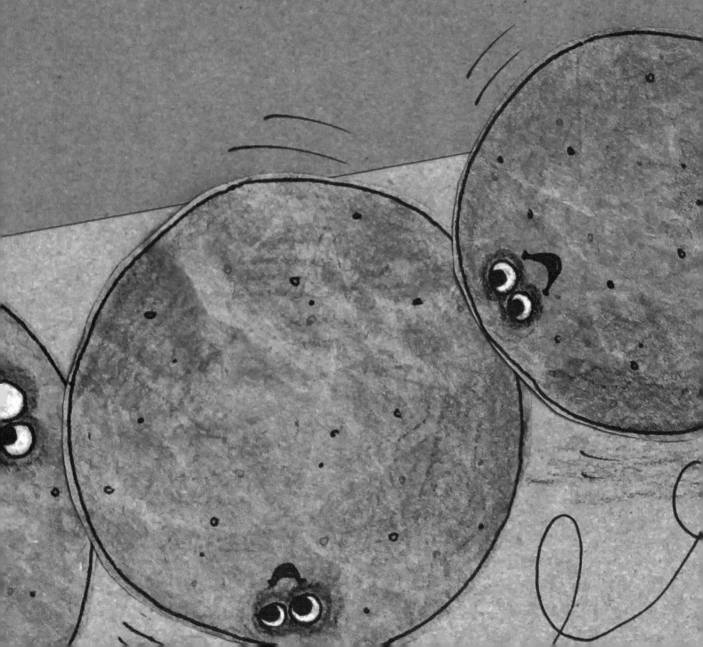

The injera rolled by a train.

እንጀራውም በአንድ ባቡር አጠገብ
እየተንከባለለ ሔደ።

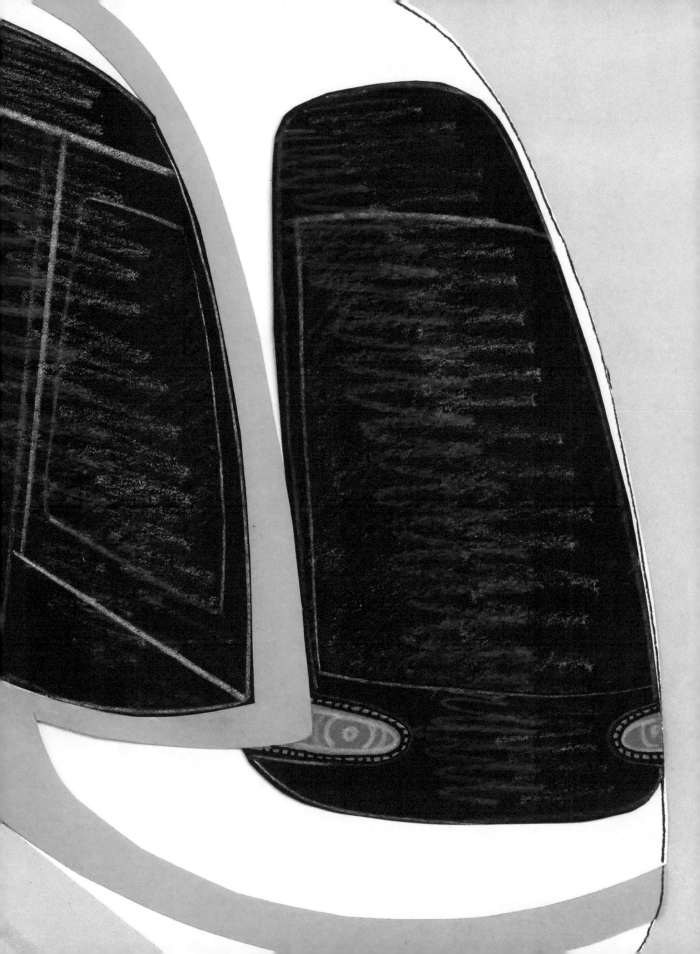

"Stop!"
people on the
train called.
"You will be soft
and warm to eat
today."

'ቁም!'አሉት በባቡሩ ወስጥ ያሉት ሰዎች። 'ትኩስ
እንደሆንክ ዛሬውኑ ትበላለህ።'

The injera called,
"You have legs,
but I am ROUND.
I roll zip-zip
across the
ground."

እንጀራውም 'አንናንተ እግሮች አሏችሁ እኔ ደግሞ ክብ
መሬት ላይ በፍጥነት እላለሁ ከብልልል ' አላቸው።

The injera rolled by three girls.

እንጀራው በሶስት ልጆች አጠገብ
እየተንከባለለ አለፉ።

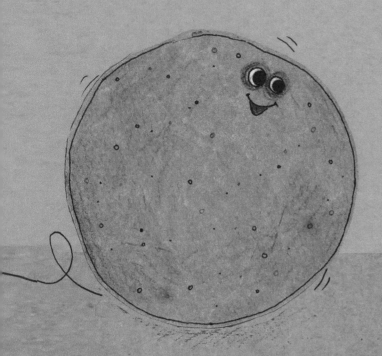

It waited for them to say "Stop!"
It waited and waited.
But the girls ignored the injera.

ቄም! እስኪሉትም ጠበቀ።
ቢጠብቅ፤ ቢጠብቅ ልጆቹ ዝም አሉ።

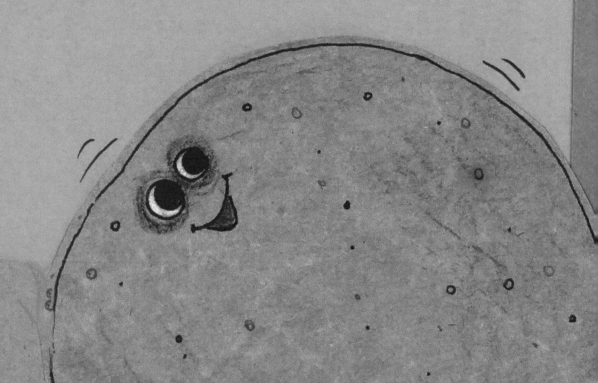

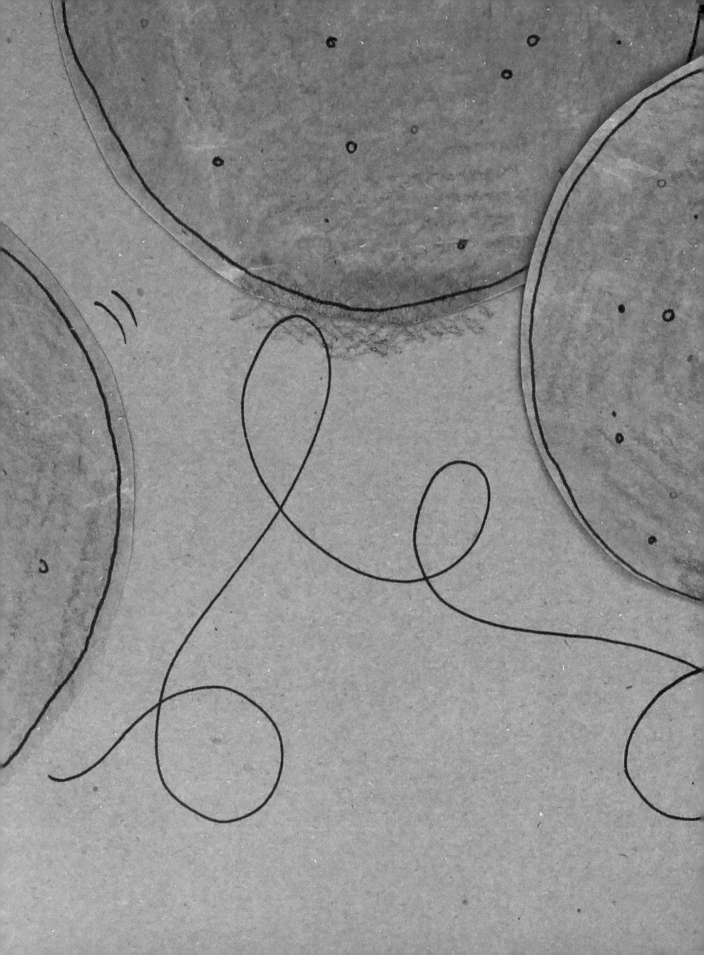

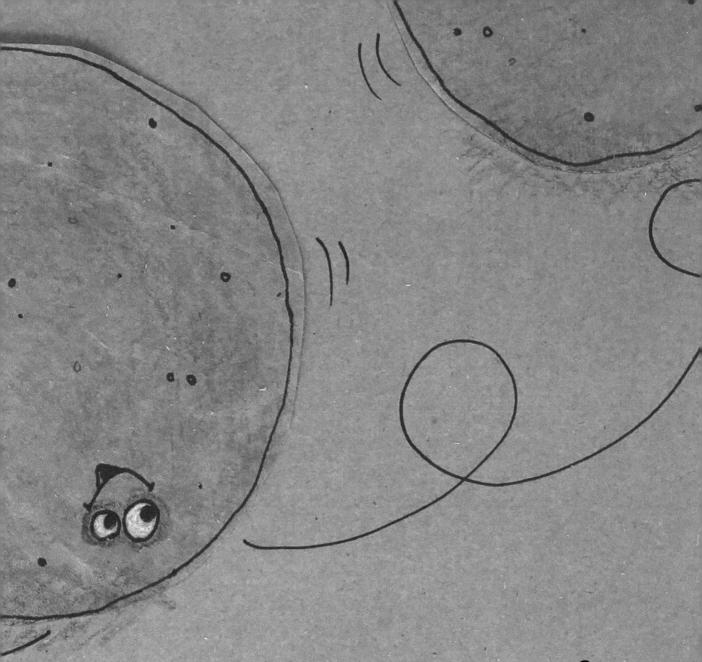

The injera called, "You have legs, but I am ROUND. I roll zip-zip across the ground."

በመጨረሻም ፤ 'እንናንተ እግሮች አሏችሁ እኔ ደግሞ ክብ መሬት ላይ በፍጥነት እላለሁ ከብልልል' አላቸው፡፡

One girl said, "You roll zip-zip, faster than a train."

አንዲቷ ልጅም እንዲህ አለቸው፤
' ከባቡሩ በላይ ፈጥነህ ክብልልል ትላለህ'

"But you are made of grain. You have no brain."

'ግን ከእህል ተሰርተህ አዕምሮም የለህ።'

She went back to reading.

ከዛም ማንበቢን ቀጠለች።

The injera rolled closer to see
what was so interesting.

እንጀራውም ምን እንደዚህ እንደመሰጣት
ለማየት ከብልል እያለ ተጠጋ።

The girl grabbed the injera.
"See?" she said.

ልጅቷም እንጀራውን ለቀም
አድርጋ 'እየህ?' አለችው።

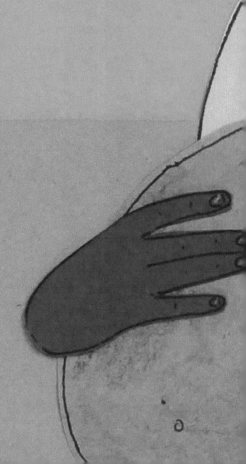

The injera was soft and warm
to eat that day!

እንጀራውም በትኩስነቱ ያን
ቀን ተበላ።

About The Story

Many Americans grow up hearing a folktale about a man made of gingerbread that runs away from a cast of characters that all join in to try to catch it. Often, the Gingerbread Man has a taunt for those running after it:

Run, run as fast as you can!
You can't catch me. I'm the Gingerbread Man!

In the end, some character (usually a fox) manages to outsmart the Gingerbread Man and gobble it up.

A version of the gingerbread man story was printed in an American magazine in the 1800s. Around the same time, readers in other countries could hear or read about a johnny-cake that rolled away (England) or a pancake (Germany) or a galette (France) or a ball of bread dough (Russia). A more recent U.S. story was crafted around a runaway tortilla.

Injera is a flat, flexible bread that is served at almost every meal in most Ethiopian households. The cook creates a batter that bubbles and has a flavor somewhat like sour dough starter. Then the batter is poured in a spiral from the outside in onto a large griddle called a mitad. The result is a large, round bread that can be used to scoop up stews made from meat, lentils, split peas, or vegetables.

About The Author

Jane Kurtz was working with Suma Subramaniam, a student in the Vermont College of Fine Arts MFA in children's and YA literature, when they challenged each other to write a story around the flat breads that are eaten in Ethiopia (Jane) and India (Suma). "Suma was an early believer in the possibility of Ready Set Go Books," Jane says. "I'm delighted that—even though it took several years—this book is now available to honor her support and encouragement of getting books into the hands of children around the world."

Jane and Suma

About The Illustrators

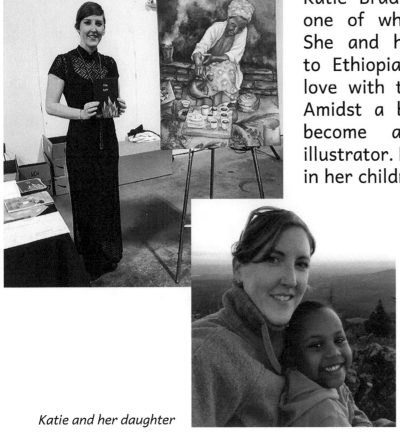

Katie Bradley is a mother of 3 children, one of whom was born in Ethiopia. She and her husband have traveled to Ethiopia twice, and have fallen in love with the country and its people. Amidst a busy and full life, she has become an artist and children's illustrator. Katie enjoys volunteering in her childrens' school and teaching art in a number of classrooms. This is her second book for Ready Set Go Books.

Katie and her daughter

About Ready Set Go Books

Reading has the power to change lives, but many children and adults in Ethiopia cannot read. One reason is that Ethiopia doesn't have enough books in local languages to give people a chance to practice reading. Ready Set Go books wants to close that gap and open a world of ideas and possibilities for kids and their communities.

When you buy a Ready Set Go book, you provide critical funding to create and distribute more books.

Learn more at: http://openheartsbigdreams.org/book-project/

Ready Set Go 10 Books

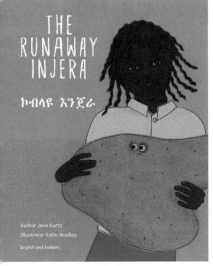

In 2018, Ready Set Go Books decided to experiment by trying a few new books in larger sizes.

Sometimes it was the art that needed a little more room to really shine. Sometimes the story or nonfiction text was a bit more complicated than the short and simple text used in most of our current early reader books.

We called these our "Ready Set Go 10" books as a way to show these ones are bigger and also sometimes have more words on the page. The response has been great so now our Ready Set Go 10 books are a significant number of our titles. We are happy to hear feedback on these new books and on all our books.

About Open Hearts Big Dreams

Open Hearts Big Dreams began as a volunteer organization, led by Ellenore Angelidis in Seattle, Washington, to provide sustainable funding and strategic support to Ethiopia Reads, collaborating with Jane Kurtz. OHBD has now grown to be its own nonprofit organization supporting literacy, innovation, and leadership for young people in Ethiopia.

Ellenore Angelidis comes from a family of teachers who believe education is a human right, and opportunity should not depend on your birthplace. And as the adoptive mother of a little girl who was born in Ethiopia and learned to read in the U.S., as well as an aspiring author, she finds the chance to positively impact literacy hugely compelling!

About the Language

Amharic is a Semetic language -- in fact, the world's second-most widely spoken Semetic language, after Arabic. Starting in the 12th century, it became the Ethiopian language that was used in official transactions and schools and became widely spoken all over Ethiopia.

It's written with its own characters, over 260 of them. Eritrea and Ethiopia share this alphabet, and they are the only countries in Africa to develop a writing system centuries ago that is still in use today!

About the Translation

Mastewal Abera is a librarian and a children 's book author who lives in Addis Ababa. She is passionate about children's literature. She came to the very first Ready Set Go Books workshop in Addis Ababa, when the team was first figuring out how to create books, and gave her translation suggestions to Caroline Kurtz—which eventually led to a new translation for The Runaway Injera.

Over 100 unique Ready Set Go books available!

*To view all available titles, search "Ready Set Go Ethiopia"
or scan QR code*

 Chaos

 Talk Talk Turtle

 We Can Stop the Lion

 Not Ready!

 Count For Me

 Too Brave

 Fifty Lemons

 The Glory of Gondar

Open Heart Big Dreams is pleased to offer discounts for
bulk orders, educators and organizations.

Contact ellenore@openheartsbigdreams.org
for more information.

CPSIA information can be obtained
at www.ICGtesting.com
Printed in the USA
LVHW072310031021
699400LV00002B/10

* 9 7 8 1 7 2 3 7 0 0 3 5 4 *